Mummy Wears a Mask

A Monster's Guide to Life...in a Pandemic

Laurie Theurer & Katie Lee Koz

Illustrations by Maria van Bruggen

Mummy Wears a Mask

Cookie Press Books

To all little monsters

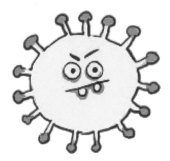

A virus arrived in Monstertown. Within a week…

Boogeyman was coughing.

Yeti was sneezing.

Werewolf was wheezing.

This caused a monstrous meltdown.

But Mayor Mummy knew just what to do.

"Don't panic!

Wash your hands!

Keep your distance!

AND WEAR A MASK!"

"Yes, a mask," said Mummy.

"I never go anywhere without mine. It's protected me through plague after plague...after plague."

But the other monsters weren't so sure.

"Serpents and spiders!" said Witch.

"How can I say my spells clearly through a mask?"

"You only use spells when you're at your cauldron. You don't need a mask inside your own home," said Mummy. "Besides, I always wear a mask and you understand what I say."

"Mgrpthugathhhhhhh!" said Ogre.

"No, I don't have any ketchup," said Mummy.

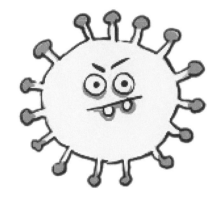

Zombie gave a double thumbs-up.

When the left thumb fell off,

he knew just how to tie it back on.

"No, no, no!" said Mummy.

"You wear them over your mouth and nose...

like this!"

"I don't vant to look vierd," said Vampire.

"No~vun vill see my beautiful face

and vonderful sharp fangs."

"Suffering scarabs!" said Mummy.

"Isn't it better to look silly than to get sick?"

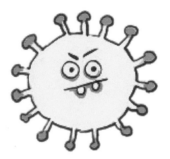

"Ah-choo!" Blob sneezed.

"Oh, no!" howled Werewolf.

"Blob has the virus!"

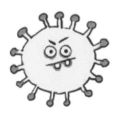

"Quick! Get Blob a mask so he won't

spread the virus!" said Mummy.

The only problem was...

nobody could find Blob's mouth or nose.

"Ve don't have enough masks

to blanket all of Blob," said Vampire.

"Vhat should ve do?"

"Toil and trouble!" cackled Witch.

"I have an idea."

"That works, I guess," said Mummy.

"But does anyone else feel a bit cold?"

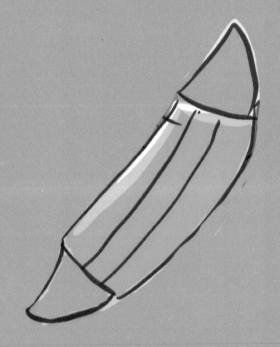

Mummy's Guide to Wearing a Mask

1. A virus is in town. You might have to wear a mask when you go out of your home right now.

2. If the mask is uncomfortable, try sewing buttons onto a headband or a strip of material, and then attaching the mask straps to the buttons. Ask an adult for help.

3. Other people will be wearing masks, too. That can look a little scary. It might also make it hard to recognize people you know. Don't worry...it's still them behind the mask. Look for other ways to recognize them, like the color of their eyes, a tattoo, or their big ears.

4. Everybody can hear you talking through your mask. Stop shouting!

5. Unless you're an Ogre, don't eat your masks. They're chewy.

About the authors:

Laurie Theurer lives in a small Swiss village where there are more cows than people. She writes stories for children of all ages and has a soft spot in her heart for funny picture books.

Katie Lee Koz lives in a big Swiss city where the people speak French. She writes for kids, teens, and adults under different names. She loves reading, writing, and buttered popcorn.

About the illustrator:

Maria van Bruggen loves to mix traditional and digital techniques to create fun and lively illustrations. She believes life is full of miracles and always tries to keep a sense of humor.

All titles in the series

A Monster's Guide to Life...in a Pandemic:

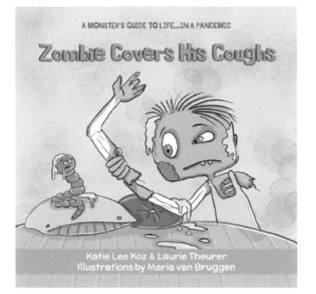

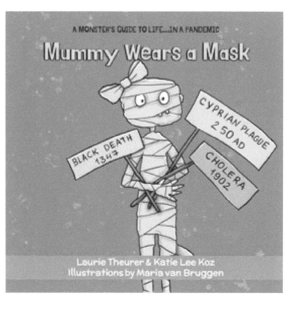

The monsters have more to learn about everyday life—from sun safety to grooming to manners to tying their shoes.

Want to be informed of other *Monster's Guides* when they are released? Sign up for our newsletter at:

www.monstersguidetolife.com

If you enjoyed this book, please leave a review.

Nonviolent Peaceforce